T.M. Cooks is the pen nam̶   ...ng collaborative writing team. The contributors are:

- Matilda Eaton

- Laila Beech

- Favour Ogbonna

- Rosie-Leigh Scally

- Millie Sharrock

- George Terry-Alway

- Mason Wilshaw

- Summer Wynne

- Lexie Knight

with cover design by Murphy Parys. The project was overseen by Joe Reddington, Dr Yvonne Skipper and Richard Seymour.

The group cheerfully acknowledges the wonderful help given by:

- Claire Woolley

- Sarah Smith

- Ruth Hamer

- Donna Armstrong

- Carolyn Lear

And a big thank you goes to Higher Horizons who funded this wonderful project. Its been a wonderful opportunity, and everyone involved has been filled with incredible knowledge and enthusiasm. Finally, we would like to thank all staff at The Orme Academy for their support in releasing our novelists from lessons for a full week.

The group started to plan out their novel at 9.15 on Monday 13 March 2023 and completed their last proofreading at 13.00 on Friday 17 March 2023.

We are incredibly proud to state that every word of the story, every idea, every chapter and yes, every mistake, is entirely their own work. No teachers, parents or other students touched a single key during this process, and we would ask readers to keep this in mind. We are sure you will agree that this is an incredible achievement. It has been a true delight and privilege to see this group of young people turn into professional novelists in front of our very eyes.

No Way Out?

T. M. Cooks

Contents

1

Chapter 1

Studying At Uni

Alice, James, Ellie, Daisy and Dave were all studying their main subject at uni. The clock ticked to 12:00, ; the bell rang for lunch and they all went down to the canteen. "Yes pizza, " they all shouted. They all went to go sit down at a lunch table. After they all ate their lunch they all went back to their main subject. Ellie was bored as she sat there in medical class. Daisy returned into her cooking class.

"No the sausages!" she shouted at another student as the sausages were burning.

"I'm sorry Daisy!"

"Just be careful or your gonna burn the school down, " Daisy was like the boss of the kitchen as she's very passionate about her skill.

Alice was studying PE because he likes athletics and sports and he also liked to do ninja moves in his spare time, James was studying Maths because he wants to have a good job when he is older, Ellie was doing medicine but she didn't want to do medicine. Daisy was doing cooking because, she wants to open her dream restaurant one day and she also has had a lot of practice since she was younger. Dave was doing Football because Dave was doing football ever since he was a little boy. Demi also wanted to be a footballer because, her dad used to always take her out to play football and her dad was always at work so it was the only time she spent with him and she also wanted to be more like her dad when she's older. They all had there speciality's and different things they are interested in.

Ellie didn't want to do medicine but wanted to be a detective. Her parents wanted Ellie to do medicine so she could be successful and the job pays well. She is also better at detective work then medical work but her parents don't believe in her that she can be a good detective. She believes she could never build up the courage to tell her parents.

Demi is a quiet girl who wants to be a professional footballer because she always went to games with her dad which made her get interested in football over time . Demi also cant speak as when she was speaking to her friend she got distracted and hit by a car. This traumatized

Demi to never speak again. Demi is rich and can buy anything she wants but doesn't as she is too scared to speak to anyone and believes she has everything she wants. If Demi doesn't become a Footballer she wants to be an actor as she thinks it will be easier as she can speak because she is not playing herself and it's pretending to be someone else. It is easy for Demi to be an actor because she has a lot of money.

Alice was a shy kid that didn't have many friends he lived with his Dad and Brother. His Dad liked his Brother more than him and thought he was better than Alice. He likes tumbling like a ninja down the stairs. He also likes mathematics and solving problems. His mum got trapped in the woods for a very long time and soon enough died that's why he's claustrophobic when he goes into the woods.

Dave is 19 and has been scouted for professional football teams. If Football doesn't work out for him he then wants to be a social worker and help people with there safety and hunger. Dave is happy but sometimes he gets a bit depressed because he doesn't have much friends because non of the people like him at school.

Daisy is good at cooking and hopes to open her own restaurant her dream restaurant would have candles on each table and would have also a breakfast menu for in the morning and her restaurant would be fancy. She began cooking when her mum had been diagnosed with cancer so she started to cook for her everyday 7 days a week. Her Dad was always working so he couldn't take care of Daisy's mum. Sometimes Daisy has to have days off school because of her mum. Daisy lives at home and travels to the University as her mum is sick.

The students love studying photography . they think it is fascinating because they get to take photos of rare and funny looking creatures they also find it amusing too with all of the nature and wildlife all around them and they really enjoy it and want to do it everyday. they really enjoy it.

Chapter 2

Who And Where?

Oliver was following TJ and Alastor hoping to catch them escaping before anyone else could, because they were very advanced and good at solving mysteries, and are good at escaping.

They all miss their family they thought they were dead. Oliver wants to see his family very bad. He never had a strong relationship with his mum or dad they were divorced so TJ never really saw his dad, he was very abusive. His mum always stuck up for him but he never really showed any love for his mum.

Oliver was anxious of the fact to find out what TJ and Alastor can do to torture the kids to make them fail miserably.

'Oh no, ' Oliver thinks, 'what if they do something brutal to them?' Oliver immediately went to work, watching and taking pictures of anything suspicious and decided to hang these pictures in visible places. He tried to get Alastor hoping that the kids will see them and he wont do anything bad to them.

Oliver had a deep connection to the forest, he

almost knew what the animals were saying and they were the only friends he had. He took care of injured animals, he loved taking their pictures. Before he came to the forest people made fun of him because he loved animals.

"If you love animals so much why don't you live at the zoo!" They would laugh, but he wouldn't let them stop him following his passion. He knew he could do better. Wandering into the forest he found an injured rabbit, he took it home, nurtured it until it was better, he used sticks as splints for it's leg!

"What are doing bringing an animal home? It won't help your future! Look at your cousin, he owns his own business and here you are bringing wild animals into the house!" His mum would yell at him. It made him feel useless.

The next day he went out to refresh his head, walking upon a beautiful forest. But he was so into the nature around him, his camera clicking away, he didn't realise how very lost he was.

But something was odd about this forest. He

swore that river hadn't been there before, he low-
ered his hand into the calm, warm water and watched
as a blue fish swam to his hand. It didn't take him
long to realise that the weather hadn't changed,
the time had stayed the same yet it felt like he'd
been in there for hours. He walked and walked,
until he came to a river. It felt like Deja vu! That
was when he realised this forest wasn't like the
others.

Alastor was suprised to see another group had
gotten into the forest, first TJ, then Oliver and
now this group of teenagers! Alastor was amazed
that they had the guts to go into this forest, so he
started to plan how he could scare them.

'Maybe I might make an earthquake, ' he thought.
'Make dead birds from the sky! Maybe I can make
a trap! Or puzzles that needs some real teamwork
to solve, things that they weren't prepared for!
Poison them maybe?'

Alastor was in a room covered in television sets
in his hut, watching every move the kids make. He
wants to make them suffer their worst fears, but

he has no idea that TJ and Oliver is watching out for him. With Oliver's pictures the kids have a chance, giving Alastor a disadvantage.

Alastor wonders if the kids have the courage to fight their monsters, as he watched the cameras as a figure appeared on screen. Oliver walked up to one of the cameras, looking into the lens.

"You promised me that this is the last one! And if it's not I will tell them everything about you." Oliver said into the camera.

Alastor rolled his eyes, 'fine, ' he thought. 'This is the last one. But not because of you, Oliver.'

Oliver is excited to see he can find out more about the group, he was curious to find out more about everyone because he wanted to see what they can do and how they can get out after all these years he's been trapped in there, he doesn't want to get out anymore but he wants to find out how he can if he ever needed to get out. He wants to see if he can help himself if anything bad happens to him so then he can get out with countless options to escape just in case he nearly gets killed like how his friends did.

He didn't want to hide from them, but thanks to his trust issues, he's hiding.

"Clack!" Oliver took another picture of the group when they were walking past.

Oliver is trying to be quiet while the group heard the sound of a camera in the distance. "Clack!" But they couldn't see anything. They continued to look around for a bit and then gave up and just decided the noise was a bird stepping on a twig.

They went on a hunt and were trying to find where the camera sound came from so they all tried to hear where it came from but they couldn't find it but all they could find is picture of an old man.

The old man has wrinkles under his eyes, he has mixed skin and thick dreaded hair, a few hairs sprouted from his chin his clothes looked strangely new but...old. Where had it come from? Alice picked it up, because he had a feeling this picture was going to be useful, putting it in his back left pocket.

Chapter 3

No Way Out?

Demi arrived first to photography club and was very enthusiastic about learning and waited for everyone to get there and learn but they found.

"Everyone's so late, " Demi mumbled to herself. She sat down on a chair and waited patiently for the other students to arrive.

Ellie was strolling down the corridor to photography club. James ran behind her

"Ellie!" James said.

"Oh hi, come on were going to be late!" They both went down to the photography club. Daisy and Alice met Demi then they all went into there room.

"Finally, " said Alice frustrated. They all got together to help each other and thought about what they there going to do for their next project.

"So any ideas?" Asked Daisy.

"Maybe we should make a statue of all of us?" Suggested Alice.

"Were in photography club, it has to be something to do with photography, " Daisy looked at Alice with a dirty look because of his thought.

Suddenly Dave burst out an idea to go in the forest and take some pictures for the presentation.

They all started to get exited to go to the forest and capture pictures of outstanding looking birds.

"Ok we need to pack our cameras to capture the birds, " said Demi. The group agreed to all pack their cameras just in case they caught something remarkable. They all started to walk to the forest everyone excited as ever.

Dave was so exited to see if he could take pictures of rare birds. He loved nature and his hobby of photography. They all walked into the forest and began to take pictures.

They all walked into the forest and took some pictures of ladybugs, birds and caterpillars. "Should we go back now?" Ellie asked.

"Yeah I think we have enough pictures now " said James.

They all turned around only to see that there was no university left, there was just trees surrounding them.

James climbed the tree and saw that we were in the middle of nowhere. He was puzzled and wasn't sure on what to do. There were no structures or buildings for miles.

"All I can see is trees I couldn't see anything else" said James.

"Are you sure? asked Ellie.

"Yes I'm positive. there was nothing else." replied James.

"Are we going to be stuck forever?" asked Demi.

"Hopefully not" said Alice.

The groups were scared for their lives they didn't know how they were going to get out of the forest. They were hopeless they though they were never going to see their families again.

Chapter 4

Flashback

TJ Was feeling hungry so he went to the forest to get some berries.

He walked and went on a hunt to find some juicy berries to eat, just the thought of berries made his stomach rumble by how hungry he is in the forest. He finds a big juicy one.

"Oooo look at this one, " he mumbles to himself. As he was distracted by the size of the berry he trips over a stick.

"Ow!" he faceplants the hard floor.

Why does life have to be so hard he thought to himself. He went to lie down beside a bush until he heard voices coming from the trees they thought it was a mysterious figure.

Alice get back in then group feeling confined from his surroundings.

Alice hates being in tight because his dead mum got trapped in the woods and died so ever since that happened he never liked tight spaces, he saw her get trapped and die so whenever he is in a tight space it brings back too much bad memories.

"What was that loud thump?" Alice asked.

"Maybe a tree branch fell down of a tree stop

being so over dramatic, " David said.

"And you wonder why no one likes you, " Alice said back.

"Sorry, " David said not caring.

"Lets stop arguing and just take photographs!" Daisy shouted.

"You're right, " James agreed. All of the group started taking photographs of there surroundings.

with confutation because the forest is unsafe.

Tj looks confused as he finds photography club taking photos as Tj thinks the forest is unsafe for people who are in it.

"New people, you have got to be kidding me, " The photography club spotted TJ amongst the bushes.

"Who's that?" Alice asked.

"How are we supposed to know?" Said Dave.

"Should we go to it?" Asked Daisy.

"Probably not, " Said Ellie.

TJ has flashbacks of when he first came into the forest with his friends it was gruesome and horrifying to his poor eyes. Tears started dripping

23

down his old, crusty eyes and wrinkled face.

Inside it frightens him. TJ has been alone for many many years and can't cope with new people entering these lands. TJ starts walking towards the group.

"Stop!" shouted Ellie.

"I'm not gonna hurt you don't worry, " The old man stuttered.

"Who are you?" Asked Daisy.

TJ went up to the group,

"Sit down, "

"No, who are you?"

"Please sit down, I'll tell you everything."

TJ starts to explain about how he got stuck in this majestic forest.

"Me and my friends went out to explore these woods and now I have fount no way out..."

"what happened to your friends?" Ellie asked.

"They went out to get some more food and got murdered, " TJ said with his head down

"By who?" Daisy asked.

"I couldn't tell you, " TJ says quietly.

TJ keeps explaining to the group how he went to the same university as them and they went to the forest to explore because of a game of truth or dare.

"That's why I don't like people, " TJ said.

The group was flabbergasted at TJ's story of how he got here.

"there's really a man in the woods that killed your friends?" asked Alice scared.

"Yeah."

"Are we going to die?!" asked Alice. Dave has never thought about his death before so this made him very scared.

"About 28 years ago me and my friends went the same school as Alastors dad. He was a new student at our school, he started to be a bit cocky and very mean to me and my friends and me and my friends thought we were the coolest in school. We tried to pick on him because he was new and had glasses and was being mean to us, we kept calling him names we would do it every single day at school until he got sick of it and tried to bully us back. But me and my friends didn't let it slide and this is how he got his revenge on me he killed my friends and almost killed me it was terrifying and that's how I got stuck in this forest. Yeah you may think its nice at the start but spend a year here and you'll see what its like."

James tells TJ apologize to him and tell him your really sorry and try be friends even if you two hate each other. It couldn't be that bad what you said to him (or could it?).TJ tells them the words he told him and they were shocked but they agreed with him because what Alastor said to him 'hopefully TJ and Alastor become friends at the end' James wondered in his head.

Chapter 5

The Split

They went in a group to find food and water for the others. Everyone was on an adventure in the forest to find food and supplies. They went in a group while Oliver was amused by watching them work together, he really wants a friendship like them but he likes to be on his own.

They needed to stick into separate groups so they wouldn't get lost. Then when they the severity of the situation, they tried to go back but were met with tall trees towering over them.

The other group need all the energy they can get ready for the day to continue there journey to find the others, so he places down food and waters to survive the next few days but hopefully they'll get out before they run out of food.

All of a sudden they split into two groups on different sides of a path. They all look around terrified but some refuse to show there true emotions towards one another they are worried encase they will never see their families again.

The groups stick together and work with each other to make sure they are all okay and not worried. The two groups felt that something was off, they knew that someone was watching them, they don't know what they want.

It made them feel scared, insecure, especially Demi. She feels like she's being watched, like there is someone hiding out there. Dave decides to stay close to Demi so that she doesn't feel lonely, which makes her feel a little bit better.

"It's okay, " Dave said to Demi, "we can look for things together! We need food after all." Demi nods her head, quietly whispering.

"Thank you."

Alastor hopes he can catch one of the groups because then he can keep them in the forest for years and wont let them escape.

Oliver took a picture of something marvellous. After years of being the forest he had never seen anything this astonishing .

He stopped taking pictures after a while because he saw them all looking around as thought they herd him so he left all the remaining photos on trees and other objects.

The group of three continued to walk in silence, awkwardly trying to figure out how there going to work together as a team when they have completely different interests

but what they do know is they needed teamwork to help each other but without the whole group everyone was left clue less.

they hoped they would be back with each other soon so they could think of ideas to get out safely without getting tricked and put into a trap.

Chapter 6

Saviour

The group were really great people for but TJ wasn't that bothered he just wants to see his son again and his mum even though he doesn't see him very much he misses his dad and mom who are divorced so he didn't see his dad very often as a child. His family life wasn't very good as he saved them and he decided to reveale himself to save the group from falling in the death hole.

Alastor was furious about this. He placed that hole to slow them down .

Alastor was mad that TJ saved them from falling into the hole.

"Why can't I trap these people!" He shouted. He looked at TJ as he helped the group get out of the hole. even the thought of TJ made him disgusted. The hole was meant for them to slow down, not for TJ to have an opportunity to save them and show he is actually a nice person.

They got saved by TJ finally revealing himself spying on them to save them the group weren't even bothered at least he saved them from falling in the pit . The hole made TJ have a flashback, to when his friend Lacey tripped and fell and he helped her back out as well but while they walked away from

Alice, James and Demi continues to travel in the majestic forest to find food and water. They kept doing this to survive. it was a brilliant method since they had no supplies. along the way they saw lots of beatiful creatures.

Then the ground caved in on its self and Demi was about to fall in the hole demi boiled up with nerves until somebody caught her just before she fell. it was TJ . Demi was glad he saved her, she was so terrified of getting lost in the hole.

After the relief of Demi being saved, James began to think he was going fall in the hole watching every step he took making sure it never went close to the hole. Because when he was young when he was younger his mum was to por

tative

Then Alice started to feel claustrophobic, the group were terrified about the hole and scared about how the hole randomly appeared. They started to wonder about what other games will appear in the forest and how dangerous these games will be and if one of the members of the gets hurt it would be devastating .

As Demi shook in fear as she remembered way she never speaks when her best friend went to the forest as she never said entering about here again as she dropped down in tears every one said, "are you ok?"

"Yes" she said as she stood up.

Chapter 7

Spy

Alastor stood there in shock. He really wanted to join in with them and have some fun. he felt very sad and unhappy because he has no friends and that is why he tries to keep them in there so he can maybe get the courage to join in but he never has. Alastor is a very antisocial person and loves helping people but he just took this job of his dad which made him stay there and live life in there.

Alastor was not expressing the surprise from TJ as he was a considerate person who loved helping out. He loves hunting and eating but was stuck there and got consumed with hatred after his father passed away.

Alastor was speechless from what he saw them all helping each over, over and over again he was really surprised by this they kept pushing and pushing each over and was really motivated to see there family again.

Alastor tried to ruining their happy moment by sending a ugly beast to destroy them. He wanted them dead at this point, he didn't want them to escape he just wanted them dead so he sent a mythical beast to defeat them but they defeated it.

Alastor felt that he would be helpless as he found out that he had no backup to help him with the group.

Alastor had no time to think so he made think harder some one had seen him already he had to think fast.

Alastor had no choice but to put them in danger but still had to give them some time he felt sad to see them dead

As they dodge the danger one of them sees a glimmer from a camera he didn't know that they know.

Alastor was left hopeless without any ideas to trap the groups in the forest he couldn't think of any ideas. He felt like he had failed.

Chapter 8

The Hidden Helper

Oliver was feeling really good about he really did give them a lot of food, water and resources Oliver kept taking photos about the wildlife and was very interested he heard a lot of them saying they misses their mum or dad and family and wanted to get home that reminded Oliver about his mum he never had a dad and hated his mum because she kicked him out of his house and really even when he was little didn't have a good relationship with his mum his dad left at a very young age his mum never had enough food for him.

He was focused on letting the group decide what to do so he kept spying on them and heard everything they said and whenever they needed food or water he always left them stuff Demi thought that it was Alastor giving them food but it was Oliver who was a good hearted person never let people beat him down he was always so enthusiastic his school life wasn't very great after he got bullied for always taking photos of thing like birds wildlife anything that was interested but somehow he always stayed happy no matter what he lover his hobby very much no one ever put him down about it .Which made him feel very good about the group and helpful he is helping them.

Alastor was furious about this but Oliver never let him get in his way and took a lot of photos to give them clues Alastor couldn't believe what he was doing he was so angry and Oliver knew this but he didn't care and kept helping them over and over again so Alastor would get more mad but this backfired on the group because he kept putting obstacles in the way of them so it would be harder to escape.

Demi wanted to say something about seeing Alastor but she didn't have the guts to. Demi was shy when it came to this. She feels left out, she wants to speak but it was like her shadow was commanding her to not speak. She could, but it felt like the force was holding her back.

When she used want to say something important she would write it on a piece of paper, but they are in the forest. So she stayed in her silence, thinking that everyone thinks that she is weird.

She wishes she could speak to her best friend, Ellie. But she couldn't, as she felt something holding her back. Maybe this wasn't the right time to speak, she had to accept this and hope that she would speak before things went wrong and it was too late.

James liked looking at wildlife and exploring nature and always wanted to bring his mum down into the woods when he was younger. He missed seeing nature, he liked looking at the birds, butterflies and the squirrels. His mum liked rabbits the best, she used to bring a bag of carrots with her into the woods to feed to them.

James feels like he is about to cry at the memory, he can imagine his mum standing there in front of him reaching out her hand out to him like she used to when he was small. He snapped out of the memory suddenly, remembering that the group was waiting for him, wiping the tears from his face.

Alice's stress left his body when he found out Oliver had clues on his camera. Though he couldn't help thinking something was wrong, because Oliver always seemed to be ahead of them and thought that maybe he was up to something. Was he part of this whole thing?

Dave was feeling sad and helpless because he missed his family and the very few friends he had. Then Dave remembered the time a shark nearly killed him and it broke him and he couldn't stop thinking about the shark and his family who he desperately wanted to see again and wants to get out of the woods.

James is very stressed with the unknown stalker who is watching them and following every step that they have taken and he didn't want to die by the stalker a he thought they were going to kill him or hurt him.so James and the rest of the group were horror-struck.

Chapter 9

Carer

The sun began to go down and the moon began to rise.

"Guys we should probably go back as its going dark, " TJ says looking up at the shimmery stars. They started walking down to TJ's base.

"This is quite a decent place, " Dave said as he's looking around the room.

"Who wants some food?" asked TJ.

"If you don't mind" said James.

TJ got all his things to set up a fire to cook some food. The group was exited to have a proper meal after a while. TJ threw a bunch of logs into the fire pot.

"That should do it, " he mumbled to himself. TJ grabbed a lighter from out of his pocket.

"Damn it, lighters out of gas."

"Don't worry I've got one, " Daisy pulled a lighter from her bag.

"Cheers, " TJ goes back in his base looking for some food to cook.

"We have no food in, " TJ aid with a disappointed face.

"Daisy why don't you go get some food for the camp?" asked Demi.

"I will but you have to come with me, " responded Daisy.

"Me?"

"Yeah, " Demi grabs her bag from of the wet grass.

"Have you got a torch TJ?"

"Yeah, here take this, " Demi and Daisy start walking down to the forest. They enter the forest. Then they go deeper.

Demi and Daisy were still inside the forest.

"Where are we even going?" Demi asked. She wished she never came with Daisy. Demi and Daisy were walking around the dark, damp forest.

"What is this?" Demi asked Daisy.

"Its food!" Daisy said with an excitable face. Daisy grabbed some berries from of the bush.

"Do you know the way out?" Asked Demi.

"Not really, " Demi's smile soon vanished from of her face. They started walking down the forest trying to remember the way back they came. While they were looking up above at the towering trees.

As Demi was walking back through the forest she kept thinking about her mum and dad and missed being at home were she was safe from the forest. She missed her twin sister and playing football with her Dad.

Demi was trying to think of things to make her happy but it just made her downhearted. Demi and Daisy spot an orange light of into the distance.

"The fire!" Daisy shout with enjoyment Daisy and Demi start running past all the trees, the rocks, and a lot of dead things.

Demi and Daisy return to TJ's base

"We got food!" shouted Daisy. TJ takes the food of Daisy and walks over to the fire. He puts the berries on the floor and places the raw meat down on the fire.

"This won't take long!" TJ told the group. He put one more log into the fire pit. The sparks fly into everyone's faces.

"Careful!" Daisy said laughing. The food was

cooked.

"Food!" TJ shouted. The group were having a laugh until Demi started to speak.

"Guys, " Demi said nervously. It was mysterious for Demi to speak. "I need to tell you all something, " everyone looked up at Demi.

"Go on, " TJ said.

"The man, I saw him, " Everyone looked up in disbelief.

"What man?" Ellie asked.

"Alastor?" TJ said.

TJ asked Demi why she didn't tell them. Demi said that she was to scared to tell them.

"I don't believe you, " TJ said.

"I'm telling the truth!" TJ walked of from Demi. Demi was upset that no one believed her. All the group kept eating their food.

Dave was eating his food thinking why it tastes weird. 'Is this food gone bad?' He thought looking at the piece of meat.

"Daisy, Demi! This food is rotten!"

"Really?" Daisy's face was in shock as she

looked down at the piece of meat in James's hand.

"Why didn't you check the food?" James shouted at the girls.

"James it was dark and cold, I don't think you would do the same neither, " Daisy shouted back.

"I would to look after the group!"

Chapter 10

Setting Up Camp

Daisy, Alice and Dave search around for a good
place to camp, Alice points to a place to settle

down and Daisy turned around quickly hoping to see the perfect place to camp but her heart sank of disappointment to see an area with bumpy grass, sludgy mud, dry leaves and rocks across the surface. Dave points out another area that was seen clearly to be be flat and empty, perfect place for them to camp .As the sun went down and frost clawed across the forest, the six started fall asleep, surrounding them was a small fire from a few sticks, a pile of school bags and 3 sleeping students.

As they wake up, a dead chicken was randomly laying in their camp spot. Daisy comes up with an idea to cook it, as they were lacking food supplies. the group started looking for something to put water in and boil the chicken.

"Would this helmet work?" asked Alice.

"Yes, it would act just like a bowl! where did you find it?" Wondered Daisy.

"Just under a few leaves." said Alice while pointing to the pile.

Daisy shuffled through to find a scruffy, old

cross-over bag that smelled like dead cats, and a black and white photo of a lady, just below the photo was a date '8th of march 1911'.

"This was a hundred years ago?!" exclaimed Daisy.

"So this forest has lasted longer than a hundred years?!" worried Alice.

"This person died in this forest a hundred years ago, we have only been here two days."

"Does this mean, we will die?!"

"No as long as we find the others we will be fine, lets just cook some chicken"

daisy grabbed some water in the helmet and re-lit the fire from last night .

she tied a few sticks together with some hard grass and put a twig through the old strap holes on the helmet. After that, Dave and Alice places the helmet on sticks over the fire while Daisy put the chicken in. The water boiled as the chicken started to roast, after it was fully-cooked they placed it down on a clean rock that they rinsed in the river to cool down .

Meanwhile, Oliver was hidden behind the tree watching them, as he prefers to be alone. He decided to take a stroll through the forest and snap a few pictures on the way. The birds whistled along with the wind that swirled around Oliver's polaroid and the rabbits hopped along with the crunch of his boots skidding the ground. Oliver loved the woods as its more peaceful and quite than the world outside the infinite forest.

After they ate all the juicy, greasy chicken. They all were so thirsty but wanted a drink that wasn't water and more flavourful.

They all sat quietly trying to think how they were going to get a drink that is not from a river.

"Wait, I remember I have James's portable cup with some tea!" exclaimed Dave

"And I have a few sugar packets that I got from the canteen, " said Alice while pulling it out his pocket.

They all sat in a circle and passed around the cup and drank it carefully thinking about what it would be like to get out of the forest and if they ever will get out.

James was thinking about his family and friends, he feels sad, worried. 'What if I never see them again?' James thinks.

"When will we get to have a proper meal or a proper drink?" said Alice

"I don't know but we'll have to deal with what we've got for now unfortunately, " replied Daisy.

James was moaning in hunger "ugh

when will this stupid food beready to eat

Chapter 11

The Medic

Ellie is hunting for food as she is stranded in a forest with no way out and has no food with her so

she gets very hungry until something catches her
eye in the corner and sees James choking hysteri-
cally on the floor like he cant breathe anymore.

She sees James lying on the floor coughing a
lot from eating a poisonous berry from the wrong
bush so she started to panic as he was so hungry
he thought he was going to pass out so he walked
over to a bush with red, blue and purple berries
on thinking they were harmless but he ate one and
felt a sudden sharp stabbing pain in the back of
his throat so he dropped to the floor struggling
to breathe as he was choking so much over a tiny
poisonous berry.

Ellie is embarrassed as she doesn't know what
to do when she sees someone chocking on the floor
and she is scared in case she does the wrong thing
and he dies, so then she

tried her best to help him and use her medical
skills to try and revive him, she opens her first aid
kit and hurry's to try find a tool to try and help
him feel better and stop choking.

Ellie hurry's to find something in her first aid

kit to help James from dying, she was glad that she thought to carry her first aid kit with her as he thought an emergency would happen in the foggy damp woods.

Ellie may feel proud of herself a she might have just saved a someone's life after he made a decision to eat a poisonous berry because he got too hungry and couldn't help eating the berry, he thought he was going to pass out he got that hungry. But Ellie also may feel scared as she might not make him better and stop choking but she said to him she will try her very best to save his life.

Ellie tried her best to save him and she finally did save him after lots of hard work trying to save his life, everyone else was also proud of her too but she was just checking if James was okay instead of listening to everyone around her, she only cared about checking if James was alright.

James looked relived after still living and couldn't stop saying thank you to Ellie for saving his life he was so grateful to Ellie. Ellie was also proud for him as he made it out alive with all of Ellies hard work she put in to trying to try save him, she was so happy that she actually saved him and everyone was thanking her all the time.

Chapter 12

Fears And Weaknesses

Alastor wanted to find out there fear so he can kill them because they are in his forest and want to get them out of there and kill them so no one will leave the magical forest and enter without leaving and he is insane Alastor got this of his dad and he loved his dad very much so he try's to kill them before they destroy the forest so no one will know about it and come in and destroy it.

Alastor wanted to finally destroy them Alastor desperately want to destroy their minds so no one will come in again and everyone will die who steps foot in there because it is that special to him he tries his best to find their weaknesses and kill them.

Alastor was feeling a bit depressed seeing a lot of friend work together because he never had any family or friends Alastor felt lonely so he decided to ruin their friendship and make them feel lonely. Alastor just wanted to make friends but because he's to evil no one wants to be his friend.

As Alaster watch in the screen he felt bad for them and wanted to make thongs more easer but he could not because he want them to learn, to defeat there enemy.

Alastor needs to try and find the groups weak spots and fears. All the group began to get ready to go to sleep.

As they drift of to sleep they all have nightmares of wat they were like before the forest wick maid them think that this mite be clows to the end of the forest then didn't now what was coming as James woke up they all say are you ok?

Chapter 13

The Revealing Silence

Alastor showed himself to Demi while walking to his invisible cabin as he knew she doesn't really speak and the others were distracted. Demi started to feel that she needed to tell the others and didn't as its reminded her of the time she decided not speak as she believed it caused her best friend to die as when she spoke to her friend and she got distracted and got hit by a car.

Demi feels scared as she is holding a secret and she knows she will never speak up and she feels like she needs to say something but believes she never will. If something goes wrong she thinks she will feel guilty and believe it's her own fault. She felt light headed and dizzy. She was anxious, which made her feel insecure. She felt unsafe. She imagined people were watching. She felt that people were taking pictures of her. She could hear voices saying 'come with me'.

Alastor felt powerful and strong. He has power to do things that other people can't do. The forest is under him. When he first arrived he was new and felt insecure. Before the forest his life was cruel. He regretted not being nice to his family, and now he has flashbacks. He remembered when he was little and he had his first hug from his mum. He cried after, because he didn't a happy kid. He was born into the type of environment where people are not nice. These were people at school. He thought that everyone around him was fake, plus he got bullied. He had only one good friend, but he moved away.

When Demi sees Alastor she hopes he is a hallucination as she does not want to speak up, she begins to wish that the others saw it too but no one said about the man and Demi realises she was the only one who saw him. She wants to believe this was a hallucination as she has been in the woods so long she might not tell the difference between what is real and what isn't real.

Alastor began to feel guilty for manipulating her into thinking that she was insane. Alastor had been in the forest for five years, and he knew how everything worked. He felt pity for her, but he knew that what he was doing was for her own good. He loved his job, but he felt bad because they were suffering.

He needed to make this as hard as he possibly can for her so she could learn and live a better life. Alastor is not living his own best life, because he is on his own. His best life would be to have friends and family. He would go out with them them and be more open. He would be generous. Sometimes he gets lonely in the forest. He imagines that there are other people around him. He doesn't want to be invisible any more.

Chapter 14

Detective

They are too nervous. And they don't want
to use there skills.

"I'll do it, " Ellie says excitable.

Ellie finally gets to do what she has always wanted to do and be a detective.

Ellie starts to try and use her detective skills.

"I'm not sure if they will work, " Ellie said nervously.

"I'm sure they will, " James said.

"yeah we will all help you to, " Daisy said with a smile.

"Thanks guys, " Ellie said.

They all start to help Ellie as they realise it will help them now and in the future.

Even though Ellie does not believe in her self the group believe in her witch is hopefully enough to

Ellie starts to think about her family and how she misses them but then she also remembers how they treated her and how they don't let her to be a detective. She misses her sister she used to find her sister annoying but now that she hasn't seen her she misses her being annoying.

Ellie try's her hardest to lead the group to

group one where Demi and James were. This means a lot to Ellie as she wants to prove her parents wrong to be a detective.

"This looks like a good place to sleep" Ellie said.

"I agree! But this also looks like a really good place to get some food". James says while licking his lips in hunger.

James and Demi looked for food whilst Alice and Ellie stayed back at the sleeping place. Demi and James found a few berries whilst Alice and Ellie set up their place to sleep.

Demi and James finished looking for food and went back to Alice and Ellie. James and Demi were back by the camp but they didn't have enough food to feed everyone so they had to ration their food.

The group were still hungry but they couldn't find anymore food. "I'm still hungry do we have anymore food?" Said Alice.

"No we don't sorry me and Demi could only find a few berries there was no other food" replied

James.

Chapter 15

The First Game

The group went to find berries and food in the
forest Dave suggested that they split up and find

as many more as they can so the group went and tasted a little bit of the berry and spit it out if it tastes bitter and disgusting but is it sweet don't spit it out and you can get more.

The group splits up to try find

All the groups sorted out where the best place where you can get berries.

It wasn't going that well James nearly eat a berry that was poisonous.

He needed to make the forest harder for the groups to get through so then he can trap them for years. The group were to good for Alastor. Alastor thought for a moment on ways to defeat them. He then thought of an idea to summon a monster to try and kill them.

He thought this would be a great idea to defeat them and stop them from getting any further through the forest and finding the way out.

They all had to help each other using their skills to defeat the monster for good and stop the monster dick from causing any damage to the forest and living things the monster is a distorted red scaly human as the monster jumps of his all fours and slashes James in the face as he punches it as it terns in to a poison's gas that gives them cuts all-over there body.

Ellie helped everyone who got injured by using some of her medical supplies even though she didn't want to she knows that she needs to help her friends get out of this alive.

James, Demi and Ellie were worried encase another monster was to come and try to attack them gain.

He was worried they would be successful and he would fail.

He needed to stop the groups before it is too late.

.

They all made a campfire and sat around it to warm themselves up because it was getting cold

they were hard times to get by.

Chapter 16

Finding Oliver

Ellie leaves the group to try to find thing like food but instead she finds Oliver who was taking pictures of a magical tree with a mouth and arms he was far away admiring the tree like monster it looked like he was friends with it he made friends with many monsters like thing taking photos with them all it looked a bit strange and Ellie confronted him off him being a monster but Oliver refuses that he is not monster he has just been here for a while and learned to talk to them.

She found him and confronted him about taking photos of monsters in a way the monster liked Oliver, he loved animals he took care of them like they were his dogs and fed them. Ellie jumped at Oliver but the monster leaped and pushed her away.

Oliver was taking photos of the other monster they killed

he found this monster interesting so he investigated it with all the photos he got of him and decided to study it and see how he got created.

Ellie was very shocked because she has never saw anyone else but the groups and he was very mysterious and was taking photos of everything and finding out new stuff

everyday and was a very intelligent person in general he was a nice person. But he was really weird because he kept taking photos and Ellie was very confused that Oliver had not ran out of camera films

Oliver revealed himself because he got found and he told everyone that he was the

person who was giving them food and water. The group was very

grateful for Oliver because he helped them to survive the wild and save them from

starvation.

Ellie is really happy that Oliver fed them and found him because he is very intelligent he will be a good asset to the group and help them survive the forest and escape.

After a while in the forest, Oliver had got lonely. He missed his family, but also loved the beauty of the forest. He took photos so he could remember the forest, and that when he went back to his family, he could show them the adventures he had. He appreciated the others thanking him, because he had helped them and he thought it was nice. It made him joyful inside.

Ellie found Oliver's suitcase full of photos and broke into it when he wasn't looking. She didn't trust him, and she wanted answers in case of him lying to them.

Oliver questioned Ellie as to way she had opened his case. As Oliver questioned Ellie. She ghosted him and didn't answer him because she never thought that she was wrong which made her loose friends because they never said when she was wrong. Ellie said" I didn't trust you, were you going to hurt us" she said to Oliver.

"Sorry for going through your suitcase you were just a bit suspicious at first because you randomly came from the forest and wanted to be friends straight away." Ellie explained

"It's alright I understand" replied Oliver

Chapter 17

Causing
Confusion

Alastor manically laughs as he thinks of terrifying ways to torture all of the people trapped in the woods, he wants to mentally hurt them and he came up with a plan to try and torture them into staying in the woods and making them fail.

He calmly thinks of ways to torture them with a big mischievous smirk on his face, as all the people think of ways to escape and get out of the misty dark woods which are very cold and muddy.

Suddenly, a big smirk appeared on his old wrinkly face as he came up with a petrifying idea which all of the people trapped in the woods will definitely not like. To make them fight their demons to make them better people.

TJ had a very puzzled look on his face as he try's to figure out what's going on because everything is all over the place and no one can figure something out. Even though he has been in the forest for 2 years, he does not know much about it, he only knows how to get around and where the best food supplies are.

Demi looks very doubtful and looks very suspicious like she is hiding something or something is wrong, but wont tell anyone because she might think they will make fun of her or not like her for telling them what's going on and the plan. she feels sad about this even though she knows what to do.

Alastor is happy as he really hopes he can cause all the groups to give up and quit trying to escape even though they wont and Alastor might fail his plan which he thinks is very good but it isn't. Alastor laughs softly to himself as he thinks he has came up with the best plan and is very proud of himself.

Demi gets sad and annoyed because nobody will believe her and she is a very quiet girl and doesn't talk a lot and is shy she also doesn't really speak to anyone as she doesn't like it and she blames herself for it which she shouldn't because its not her fault she could also feel very overwhelmed with everything what's going on.

(In Demi's head) "Oh no maybe I should've spoken earlier or else none of this would've happened!" and she thinks he has done something wrong by not speaking up and being shy when she doesn't say anything to anyone and she blames it all on herself.

Chapter 18

The Set Up

Alastor took most of the students' food and
valuables. This created an argument between the

group and they fell out for a bit. He used small robot animals to take their things while they were sleeping. He had a remote control for them. He felt good because it is fun to watch a fight. Daisy was the first to wake and to notice something was missing. Her water bottle was gone. She looked everywhere for it. James was the next to wake up. Daisy asked James, 'Have you seen my water bottle?'

"What does it look like?"

"Pink with little flowers."

James was shaking his bag looking for something. "Have you seen my wallet?" he asked.

"No, and why do you need a wallet in the forest?"

Alice woke up. He couldn't find his phone.

"Can someone call my phone?"

"There is no signal in here, " whispered Demi.

Oliver said, "There is a thief in in the group."

"Everyone wake up!" said Daisy. "Where is my stuff?"

Everyone wakes up.

"Why did you wake us up? We were sleeping,
" said TJ.

Daisy replied, "We all know you stole our stuff.
You and Oliver. You're strangers. Why should we
trust you?"

TJ said, "Have some pity. You've met some
new people."

Demi, too afraid to speak, thinks it might be
the strange person she met, but she is too afraid
to say anything.

They had a big argument. Two people were
fighting. Demi pointed in the direction she last
saw Alastor, but she was too shy to say anything.

"You thief, how dare you?" he shouted at
James.

James swore back. "It wasn't me. If you don't
believe me, check my bag.

They had lost their food. They were arguing
about food problems the groups searched everywhere for safe berries to eat as they are searching
they spot water.

TJ said, "There might be fish in that lake. We

can make fire and cook the fish."

Daisy took a lighter from her pocket. She decided to hide it as she didn't trust anyone. She thought there might be someone watching them, so she decided to keep it on her.

TJ and Oliver had lived in the forest a long time and had caught fish before. They already had found a metal pot. Daisy used it to take water from he lake so she could boil it later.

James got VERY angry and started throwing stuff around. They all tried to calm him down and stop him from breaking things but he was too mad to calm down. This was because he still couldn't find his phone. He then realised that TJ and Oliver had been there a long time so life doesn't depend on gadgets.

Demi feels bad because she hasn't said anything yet and she has been letting the whole group down. people think there is something off with her.

Oliver asks her, "Why aren't you speaking? Why are you hiding from us?"

"She isn't hiding anything. She is too shy to speak, " said Alice.

Demi wanted to talk about the man she saw, but she kept it in, because she thought Alastor might ruin her career. She doesn't know anything about him.

"Who took all the food and water?" Ellie shouted

"It wasn't me replied James

"Well then who was it?" Ellie said whilst raising her tone

"I don't know why are you asking me?" James shouted back

"Guys stop fighting its nobody's fault maybe a fox got into the food and water or something but whatever it is it doesn't matter right now all we need to worry about is trying to find food and water. Demi Ellie and James you go try to look for some water whilst me Daisy and Dave try to look for some type of food." Alice interrupted.

Ellie, Demi and James (group 1) all went to go look for some water whilst Alice, Daisy and

Dave (group 2) went to look for some food. Group 1 couldn't find much food they could only find a few berries. Although Group 2 couldn't find any water throughout the forest and felt hopeless because they were losing all their energy.

Alastor is getting annoyed at how quickly the groups are getting through the tasks.

"I need to make this harder for them they are getting through the tasks too quick I need something bigger and better to stop them" Alastor thought to himself.

"I need to make them argue more and split up again then they'll definitely never make it out then" Alastor corruptly thought to himself.

Chapter 19

The Secrets

Sooner or later, Ellie spots Oliver and points
for him to come over to the group.

The group are confused on how she knows this person and Ellie explains she met him when she parted from the group and he has been in the forest for some time .

"hi.." muttered Oliver.

The group awkwardly greeted him back.

Dave asks Oliver if he knows if anyone else is in the forest.

"Not in person" replied Oliver.

"What do you mean by that?" asked Daisy.

"I have seen a strange man who always wears a cap in some of my photos, but I do not know who this man is" questioned Oliver.

Demi starts to wonder why Oliver was following them as she already knows of the strange man and his invisible cabin. She begins to wonder if Oliver is being creepy and stalking them but also remembers he could generally be a man in the woods who just lives there.

Oliver pulls out a group of photos with the same man in each of them wearing the same scruffy old clothes that he seem to have grown out of. The group gathered around to look at what Oliver has shown them.

"who else could be in the forest!?" wondered Dave.

"could it be a ghost" replied Ellie.

"Or a reflection possibly" added James.

"I'm pretty sure no one in this group knows this man, " said Daisy

Demi knew all about this strange man and maybe where his bunker is or where he lives but she cant say anything about it as she cant speak. She felt annoyed and frustrated about that she cant use her voice, but also pressured as when ever the group asked about the man, she knew but could not say anything. she would never think she could build up the courage and confidence to say anything but she knew she had to say something.

Everyone was chatting while Demi was getting more nervous waiting for herself to have courage. She wanted to speak but it felt like every time she tried something would shut her mouth back closed

"I have seen the man in the photo he lives in this weird invisible cabin not far from here" screamed Demi as all her words rushed out at once.

Demi felt more confident after she used her voice

"YOU CAN SPEAK?!" exclaimed Ellie

the group was so happy Demi found her voice but flabbergasted that she could speak

"You knew all this time and you didn't tell us?" said Daisy as she felt Demi didn't want to help

"Hey, don't blame it on her, she couldn't speak that is not her fault." replied Alice

"I'm sorry for not saying anything but shouldn't we be finding this man he could know something about getting out" added Demi.

The group agreed and they all began to help search for the invisible cabin with Demi.

Chapter 20

Building Up A Plan

In the distance, Daisy spotted a shiny, blue lake.

"A lake!" Daisy shouted. They all walked up to the lake. A brown thing stood in the lake.

"What's that?" Dave asked. They all looked over at the brown thing in the water. Oliver walked over to the edge of the lake.

"Hmmm, " Oliver looked down at the cabin.

"What's up?" Ellie asked. Oliver recognises that cabin.

"Iv seen that cabin before." Oliver grabs his camera.

Oliver was in disbelief "How did I miss this?" Oliver said.

"Miss what?" Ellie asked. Oliver looked back up to the cabin.

"The cabin, its in my photo, " All the group looked at Oliver.

"Well what should we do?" asked Daisy.

"maybe we should go over to the other side, " TJ suggested.

"And how are we gonna to that?" Asked Dave.

"maybe we should just leave it and go." Demi said. Demi cant swim and she is scared to tell the others.

"That's a terrible idea, " Ellie said looking at the cabin. Because Ellie liked detective work she wanted to explore the cabin.

"Guys can we just go and explore something else."

"Why?" Asked Daisy.

Demi thinks that she is letting the team down and realises that she needs to tell them that she can't swim but she is to scared to do so. She thinks for a little. And a little more. Until she decides to own up to everyone.

"G-Guys, " Demi stutters. She looked down. She thought about her decision for a moment. She decides to just say it.

"I can't swim." Fear filled up in her body as she said the words that she thought she would never have to say. She was scared that the group was going to make fun of her for not being able to swim.

97

"Oh, why didn't you say so?" Said TJ. Fear left Demi's body as she was relieved that no one made fun of her.

"We will stay behind for you, " James said with a little smile on his face.

"Really?" Demi said.

"Yes of course were a team, "

"Thank you for staying with me, " Demi replied. TJ and James decides to stay with Demi as they are all a team.

"how are we going to get across?" Asked Demi. James thought for a while.

"We can build a raft!" TJ shouted.

James started gathering supplies for the raft as the rest of the group starts swimming across the lake. James needed to gather as much supplies as he could. The rest of the group made it to the end of the lake.

"Oliver, look at that photo again, " said Daisy. Oliver pulls out his camera from out of his ruck sack.

"Look at that hut!" Daisy takes the picture

from Oliver.

"What hut?" Daisy's face had a confused look on it. Oliver takes the picture back of daisy.

"This hut, " Oliver points at the Hut on the picture. Little does he know only he can see the picture.

"I can't see it, " Daisy said. Oliver was confused on why only he could see the hut.

"How am I the only one who can see the hut on the pictures why can no one else see the hut?" said Oliver with a confused look on his face.

"What is happening?"

Chapter 21

Confronting Alastor

"Where is my son?" TJ shouted.

As the group finds Alastor they all charge in anger "where is the way?" TJ screams "where is my son?" As T.J knew that he had his son.

As they confronted Alastor with anger in there eyes they were very annoyed by Alastor so they confronted him and found him, they all wanted to kill him and escape the forest as Oliver says don't well be as bad as him.

Alastor wasn't expecting them as he didn't know how they saw the cabin as he explains that only he is meant to see the cabin. A fight breaks out between James and Alastor.

Demi was really overwhelmed because she knew the whole time and finally she burst she felt sad and lonely and she couldn't comprehend what was happening around her. this made her feel awful.

Suddenly Demi's head filled with thoughts and sad moments from her life he couldn't think about anything else only how her best friend died and disappointing the whole group and letting them down. She forgot she was in the forest . She just couldn't stop thinking about how she let the group down and how much time she has been spending in the forest.

"When am I going to see my parents and siblings again? . Why didn't I tell the group that I saw him?. Why can't I speak up? Why am I always the one who is too scared to do anything?" Demi thought .

"When am I going to see my parents and siblings again? Why didn't I tell the group that I saw him? Why can't I speak up? Why am I always the one who is too scared to do anything?" Demi thought.

Demi never had a breakdown but today was the day that she couldn't stop thinking of everything that makes her sad and frustrated.

The whole group could tell that Demi was worried and sad so Ellie went over to Demi and started to comfort her "It's okay Demi. We are all here for you " Ellie said.

"You have done the right thing to speak up, " Alice smiled, "maybe we should stop asking her questions guys." Alice wanted to make Demi feel more comfortable.

"Maybe we should take a rest, " TJ said.

The group stopped fighting and started to help each other again and help Demi feel better.

Demi got up and started to feel a little bit better "sorry" said Demi.

"It's okay" Ellie said.

"We are sorry for shouting and arguing, " James said.

They all decided to stop arguing from that point and started caring more about themselves and the others.

They had defeated their demons, they were happy but they were still worried about the shy girl.

Chapter 22

Freedom?

The group were exhausted after defeating their fears.

"Come on follow me!" Alastor shouted.

"Where are we going?" Daisy replied back.

"Leaving this place" he said while running.

"Oliver are you coming or what?" Oliver stood their silently with tears in his eyes.

"No I will stay!" Oliver shouted.

"What wrong?" TJ said confused.

"I just want some time alone, " Oliver said.

"Are you sure?"

"yes I am, yes I am sure."

Oliver is positive that he wants to stay .

His mum makes him very upset and discourage when he was at home and treated him in the worst way. He also wanted to stay because he wants to take a lot of photos of the forest.

"But why?" Dave asked Oliver with confusion on his face

"I'll be fine, it's okay" Oliver replied.

"You cant stay here, " Alaster said

"I'll be okay, " Oliver said but then he have to see his mum .

"Wait Oliver were going to go and have a group

discussion, " James told Oliver.

"For what?" Oliver asked confused

"If you can help us, " the group went in into a circle

"Ok I don't know if Oliver should help us because he's a bit strange, " Daisy said

"Don't forget about the fact he's been alone for most of his life, " Dave added

"Yes but he's a nice guy and he might be able to help us get out of here, " The group carry on discussing about if they should let Oliver help them get out. After a while, they went back down to Oliver

"So can I?" Oliver asked the group. The group told Oliver that they don't know if he can.

But Oliver started to explain to them that he wanted to help people overcome their fears.

"I want to stay here my mum was very abusive and because this is an endless forest I can take as many pictures as I want and I will also come out of the forest when I am ready." A tree fell "BANG!".

"Oliver you have to help us, " They all start

107

walking until they stumbled across a dark room.

"I don't know but it looks like a hut, " replied Daisy

The group were confused about why there was a dark room. They weren't sure for how long it had been there or what was in it but they were very perplexed.

Chapter 23

Personal Monsters

Oliver stood there patiently waiting for the next person to show up to help them with the tricky game they have to solve. The game was very hard it was like it was impossible. Alastor was laughing.

The monsters ran at them with a malice smile on there face Oliver tried to help but he had to stay behind, he was very scared for them, he thought they would die as there monster's were very scary, TJ's monster was his son because someone took him away from TJ and he thought his dad abandoned him but he just got taken away by people and never saw his son again so his biggest fear is him seeing his son again and living with the guilt of letting his son go.

He is distraught by the sight of his son he had to give up the guilt fast or he would be taken away. He and his son had a very good relationship, they used to play catch and play in the park together he loved his son but suddenly when he left his son for 5 minutes, he came back and he was gone. He was so sad about this, he always thought that it was his fault that his son is gone.

James's monster was his abusive dad, as soon as he saw his dad he went into tears straight away, this reminded him about his mum and dad's divorce. He never saw his mum very much he lived with his dad, who was a drunk man and always used to beat him for no reason and never did anything ever to his dad. He was a horrible man.

Dave has a horrible fear of water that's why he is scared of sharks. He tried to swim once but he saw a shark and now he is terrified of them his dad got bitten by a shark once and never took him swimming or in the sea ever again. His relationship with his mum wasn't that good he mostly went to the park with his dad because his mum was always busy working, cooking or cleaning and stressing about little things, his dad always made time for him it didn't matter what he was doing. The shark came flying at him and he barley missed it the floor turned into water and he couldn't swim but he started swimming and found out that he could actually swim very well and he kicked the

111

shark and swam down to some glass and broke it so he could defeat his monster and eventually did.

Demi's fear was her big speech she is having in 2 days at her university. The monster pushed her through a door and she had an illusion that she was doing her speech, she stood up on the stage and placed the microphone to her mouth ready to speak, sweat poured down her face splashing on the dusty floorboards as she tried to speak the monster rushed in and she was almost strangled to death, her life flashed before her eyes of her child-hood always being picked on for being so quiet but suddenly the crowd shouts for her to speak and she did she did the speech and defeated the monster and the monster just vanished and let go off demi everyone was so proud of her and they were happy she could survive it and spoke up because that was always her biggest fear in life and now the group finds her annoying because she speaks to much.

Ellies monster was her mum and dad and she had to say and stand up to herself that she doesn't want to be a doctor she wants to be a detective instead she was scared at first but suddenly everyone outside was cheering her on and she really didn't want to.

"I DONT WANT TO BE A DOCTOR!" screamed Ellie from the top of her lungs.

"I want to be a detective instead!" she added.

Her mum and dad just suddenly disappeared and defeated her monster once and for all.

Daisy's biggest fear was spiders. At first their was nothing but silence, then she heard the slight sound of spiders crawling and getting louder and louder. Then it stopped. A big spider jumped out and crept up to her. She slammed her self against the wall hoping to avoid it. The spider didn't want to harm her at all but she needed to notice that. It crawled up in a corner trying to start make a web. Daisy started to feel peace with it as she could see their was nothing to be scared about and the spider faded away and Daisy was back with the group along with the others.

Alice's biggest fear was small spaces and deep

water. he was always scared of deep water and small spaces because his mum died from small spaces and he is scared of Alligators attacking him in deep waters. But then all of a sudden Alice was in a room that was getting smaller with water filling the room every 2 minutes . He started to panic and shake with fear, he was terrified for his life. After a while he started to hear loud swishing noises in the water next to him. He rushed over to the other side of the room but the noise followed him. He stayed in one corner if the room and waited there but after he stopped a shark appeared out of thin air and started swimming around the room but it didn't want to hurt him the alligator wanted to befriend him. Alice then realised that Alligators weren't that scary. The alligator disappeared and Alice was back with the other students.

"YES WE DID IT" Demi screamed with excitement

"I cant believe We defeated our personal monsters that was the scariest time ever " Dave replied

"We all did great even though we weren't their for each other we still overcame our fears all on our own." James proudly said. The students were all proud of one another for defeating their monsters and overcoming their fear with whatever it was. They couldn't wait to celebrate overcoming their fears.

Chapter 24

The Escape

Alastor, Alice, James, Oliver, Ellie, Demi, Daisy, and Dave (both groups) get the courage and to finish defeating their monsters They were all very scared inside but they had to be brave to get out of there.

"Lets stick together and help each other no matter what." Dave said.

All of them came up with a plan and tell the others about what they are going to do They all made a plan and told it to each other quietly .

They see the exit right in front of them and they jump for the exit in hopes it isn't a trap

They are filling up with excitement and happiness.

"I cant wait!" said James

as Oliver says "I will stay behind as Alister said there needs to de another game maker see you we I am out by." As they all argue about it Oliver pushed them in.

All of the students were exited to see how there family were doing they couldn't wait to go home all of them were exited to go home as they forgot what it feels like to sleep on a bed.

They didn't know how much they could've come

together all because of a forest.

They all ran excitedly to the exit and couldn't believe how close they've gotten with each other they didn't know how much they could've come together all because of a forest.

The groups couldn't believe how much hard work they've been doing to escape the forest and how much they have gotten along with each other.

the group couldn't believe they made it out. now they could all full fill their dreams

"I can't wait to go home and see my family" shouted Demi out of excitement

" I'm going to go to Mac Donald's first I'm really hungry" replied James

They all finally escape the infinite forest after lots of hard work the group couldn't believe they made it out. now they could all full fill their dreams.

Chapter 25

When Dreams Come True

They are all very happy with their brand new live, they never thought they would get the chance to live in.

TJ is now an actor and spending a happy life with his son and his wife.

TJ is now very joyful living in his happy life with his son and wife he also makes a lot of money being an actor in a high paid job that gives a lot of money as actors get put into films.

Alice is now a famous athlete who plays in the Olympics for England and has a world record in javelin, hurdles, high jump, long jump and the three hundred metres race!

James is living the best life he could ever imagine, he is famous and has lots of money from fighting in the MMA, his mum also beat cancer! He was so proud of her for beating it and she continued to live a good life with him.

Oliver enjoys the forest and he likes taking photos of things in his spare time, he is waiting for the next person to show up at the forest to help them with the tricky traps in the deep, damp woods which you could get lost in easily.

Ellie's parents were forcing her to be a doctor and to study medicine but she doesn't want to she wants to be a detective, she also doesn't like this as she doesn't want everyone just to think of her as someone who is a Doctor or study's medicine and can always help people with injury's.

Demi got to be a pro footballer in the championship playing for Stoke City FC and being a top goal scorer in the WSL league and is now very happy her her mum and dad are very proud.

Demi is feeling satisfied with her life as she is probably making a lot of money as well she is very good at football and feeling great about her new career, she used to never talk but now she talks to everyone as she has finally stopped being shy and loves talking.

Alastor has started being much nicer so now he has made a lot of new caring friends who love him, now he is living a very joyful life which he had always dreamed of.

Daisy is happy in her life as she has achieved

her dream and became a great chef who cooks amazing food for well known people across the countries and is now very rich over the delicious amazing meals she cooks for people she even cooks 5 star meals for celebrates. She is now the one of the world best chefs.

Dave got to be a star player for Manchester City FC becoming the Premier Leagues top goal scorer and wining the champions league and the FA cup by scoring a hattrick on his debut but Dave used to be shy and not talk to a many people but now he has realized he has got to speak up and make new friends because if he is a footballer as you should get along with the other people to play he made lots of new friends, he has now became rich and is very happy living his dream life no one thought he would make, it he is also very proud of himself for becoming a pro footballer and even was making over 300K a month!

Chapter 26

Mysterious Disappearance

After some time (2 years) they decided to meet up and visit their long lost friend Oliver since he was there to take care of the woods for 2 years, so they agreed to bring some stuff for him as a thank you.

2 years later the photography club went back into the forest to go visit Oliver. They were all excited to go and see there old friend. They all agreed to go and get some gifts for Oliver as he has stayed behind and looked after the forest for all that time. Daisy, Dave, Ellie, Alastor, TJ, James, Demi and Alice met up at the university.

"I am so exited" said Demi with hope that they are going to see Oliver but what they did not know that there was something unexpected for them waiting in the woods. What is not Oliver!!! They started to make there way through the forest.

"what's that? "Alice said

"but he was the only one in the forest" Demi said

with Courage Daisy picked up the picture and

felt goose bumps shiver through her hands. They all had a bad feeling that there was some one else other than Oliver. As soon as they saw the picture, their body's froze in shock. Then Daisy immediately dropped it from what was in it.

They make their way through the woods with an unpleasant feeling of danger until they saw weird foot prints appear in the wet mud so they decided to follow it but it was the worse idea they have ever made.

Few minutes passed and they saw weird looking red things Ellie "BLOOD!" they all got goose bumps and they all ran as fast as they could until they had a big distance from the blood.

Alice felt more claustrophobic as they went further but nothing will stop him because it will remind him of his mum because she died here. Then they heard a loud cry which went on for 30 seconds and suddenly stopped.

James picked up a picture of a dead person covered in a with white sheet with his body covered in blood and maggot crawling over it and the person was his old friend and had memory's of him and Sam in a park with it was the last place they met.

They looked down at the picture "Oliver? can you hear us?" they looked around them but there was nothing, was it was a trap? Oliver was no where to be seen could it be a monster? "Oliver, Oliver where are you can you hear us hello is any-one there." James said while shaking in fear.

Ellie used her detective skills by trying to look for footsteps to find a bit more evidence to try find about where Oliver went.

Could it be the cannibals? Or did he escape himself? Or has he died? The group were anxious and scared, frightened for his safety.

Where is Oliver...?

Printed in Great Britain
by Amazon